Whipsnade
or
Bust

Jeannie's Crab Lake Winter Tales

David Mulford

Illustrated by
Christine Cathers Donohue

BROWN BOOKS KIDS

While the human characters and the places in this book are drawn from life, this is a
work of fiction. The events and circumstances of this book are wholly imaginary.

Jeannie's Crab Lake Winter Tales

Brown Books Kids
16250 Knoll Trail Drive, Suite 205
Dallas, Texas 75248
www.BrownBooksKids.com
(972) 381-0009

A New Era in Publishing®

Publisher's Cataloging-In-Publication Data
Names: Mulford, David C., author. | Donohue, Christine Cathers, illustrator.
Title: Jeannie's Crab Lake winter tales / David Mulford ; illustrated by Christine Cathers
    Donohue.
Description: Dallas, Texas : Brown Books Kids, [2019] | Series: Jeannie's Crab Lake ;
    [2] | Interest age level: 004-008. | Summary: "Jeannie has come back to Crab Lake,
    Wisconsin with her family, like she does every winter. She and all the woodland
    creatures around the lake will partake in great fun, mischief and adventure, and
    you can read all about it in these five sweet tales."--Provided by publisher.
Identifiers: ISBN 9781612542782
Subjects: LCSH: Winter--Juvenile fiction. | Forest animals--Juvenile fiction. | CYAC:
    Winter--Fiction. | Forest animals--Fiction.
Classification: LCC PZ7.1.M85 Jew 2019 | DDC [E]--dc23

ISBN 978-1-61254-278-2
LCCN 2019935227

Printed in the United States
10 9 8 7 6 5 4 3 2 1

For more information or to contact the author,
please go to www.DavidMulfordBooks.com.

Dedication

To my beloved Jeannie, who loves Crab Lake; dear Kathleen, who always knew animals can talk; and to Jason Roberts, whose artistic talents and construction skills made the log cabin at Molly Point a reality.

Acknowledgments

I would like to acknowledge the kind and dedicated efforts of Sherry LeVine and her colleagues at Brown Books in bringing out two books and six stories about my wife Jeannie and all her animal friends and their adventures at Crab Lake, Wisconsin.

I also want to acknowledge the extraordinary work of Christine Cathers Donohue, whose illustrations capture so beautifully Jeannie's woodland friends in their Northwoods home.

Finally, I would like to recognize the patient efforts of my assistant, Deanne Breunig, in preparing my stories annually over so many years.

Return to Crab Lake

Jeannie was very excited. She and David were off to Crab Lake for Christmas. Jeannie had told the cardinals in the holly tree in the garden, and by this time, surely the news had traveled all the way to Wisconsin. Jeannie was sure she would soon see all her forest friends at Crab Lake.

The snow lay deep and heavy on South Crab Road. The Blazer soon bogged down and could make no further progress. Jeannie climbed out into the cold, dark stillness. She stood, listening—listening to the bark of the wolf cubs and the sound of fresh snow sliding off the pine boughs.

Suddenly, she saw movement beside the trees. At first, she thought that a large snowball was rolling slowly toward her from the woods. Then it stopped, and she saw that it was a small, furry animal—more precisely, a small bear.

"Pudgey!" Jeannie exclaimed. "How wonderful to see you after a whole year! But Pudgey—what are you doing here?"

"Er-uh, er-uh—" Pudgey shifted from foot to foot, panting hard from his exertions in the snow. "Uh-er—waiting for you. Waiting to help you get to Molly Point."

"But that is four miles down the road," said Jeannie.

"I know," Pudgey puffed. "That is why we are here—all of us and the sleigh." He beamed as he shuffled about in the snow.

Then Jeannie saw the other animals in among the trees behind Pudgey. They were all there—Frog, Bug, Loon, Mole, Squee-Squee, Alfred, Boulder, Otter, Grey Beard, Chuck, Leaper, Lounger, Munk, Chip, Charles, Gladstone, Heron, Wolfie, Porky, Piney, Prockey, Dasher—and there in the rear was Mr. O'Possum of Lynx Bay.

"Oh! You are all here! After a whole year . . ."

There was shuffling, coughing, and growling as the animals moved around.

"You saw most of us last summer," Pudgey pointed out. "Isn't that so?" he said, poking Mr. Woodchuck with his elbow.

"Indeed, that is quite true," said Mr. Woodchuck in his best Claridge's voice.

"But we did not speak then," said one of the deer, "so it doesn't count."

"Why not?" shouted an otter as he slid by in the snow, chased now by two other otters.

Nobody paid any attention to the otters.

Then Mr. O'Possum of Lynx Bay stepped forward. He was his usual serious self. "Technically, of course, Pudgey, Mr. Woodchuck, and the otters are right. But after all, it is talking and playing together in the woods that truly brings us together."

There was a cheer. The matter seemed to have been settled, and now Jeannie was surrounded by all her animal friends.

Jeannie clapped her hands. "It is so wonderful to be back and to see you all again."

The animals began unloading the Blazer. Jeannie and her husband David helped. It kept them warm in the freezing night air. Soon the sleigh was piled high with bags and Christmas boxes.

"We'll have to choose a Christmas tree too," squealed Jeannie, now far too excited to be polite. She began to dance with the animals in the deep snow. The big bears lumbered about, and Jeannie grabbed their heavy fur and hung on for a ride. The bears did not mind a bit, and the smaller animals jumped and rolled about in the snow. Others climbed the trees—the squirrels, porcupines, bear cubs, possums, and raccoons. The deer leaped high in the air, showing off their white tails, and the beaver, otters, woodchucks, skunks, rabbits, and others rushed around, getting underfoot.

Soon they were all exhausted and out of breath in the snow. But when they had recovered, Pudgey shouted, "Let's go to Molly Point!"

With that, Jeannie, David, and most of the small animals scrambled onto the sleigh. Like he had before, Mr. Woodchuck took the driver's seat. He turned around to make sure that everyone was safe and secure.

"I am going over Hurst Lake and then up through the birch forest, so you will need to hang on," he said.

Up on the driver's seat next to Mr. Woodchuck was Mr. O'Possum in his red wool lumberjack coat, with his long, pink tail winding off the seat and into the sleigh.

Woodchuck tapped the deer, and they were soon underway, smoothly and silently but for the soft bells on the harnesses of the deer. It took but a moment to cross Hurst Lake, and soon they were among the silent white birch trees, climbing to the top of the hills.

As the sleigh started down, there were shouts of approval from the animals. The larger animals ran behind the sleigh in the snow. Up and down the small hills of South Crab Road went the sleigh, passing the Beaver Pond on the right, which lay in deep repose under the ice and snow. Over the snowy hills and under the snowy trees the sleigh slid until it finally stopped at Molly Point. Out piled all of Jeannie's friends. "Come to the lake," they shouted, and together they waded downhill through the deep snow to the point.

There in the moonlight lay the wide expanse of snow covering the frozen lake. Ridges of crusted snow spread out like waves, and the wind stirred the light powder which had gathered on the surface. The cedar trees' deep green tops stood out against the sky, and their gray trunks blended with the shadows of the woods.

The bank sloped gently onto the surface of the lake, and the snow lay deep like a warming blanket over the soft, mossy earth and the billions of packed pine needles. There was no sign of human life—not a single track or footprint in the snow. Jeannie stood, gazing out at Dick's Island and the far shore, dark in the distance against the violet sky and the brilliant stars.

Early the next morning, it snowed. The snow continued with a steady fall of large flakes throughout the day, making the south side of Crab Lake completely inaccessible by road. That evening, the snow stopped, and the temperature plunged well below zero. Deep under the snow, under the roots of the great pines and birch trees and tucked behind the gnarled roots of the cedars, along the banks of the streams, every den, cave, and burrow was packed to capacity by the small animals of the forest, while Jeannie and her family stayed snug in their cabin.

Jolly groups of moles, squirrels, rats, mice, rabbits, woodchucks, hedgehogs, badgers, beavers, otters, and many others were gathered in brightly lit caverns around roaring fires, drinking hot Christmas punch and eating delectable nuts and bits of stewed birch bark. Outside, the deer nestled deeply in the new drifts, and the bears had their own gathering in one of the large dens provided by an uprooted white pine. Even the owls, sitting high in the trees, visited quietly as they watched for the rising of the moon.

Christmas Eve Day broke clear and cold. The animals were out at dawn, and preparations were made to cross Crab Lake to Presque Isle Road, where Jeannie and her friends would meet all the families coming for Christmas. By midmorning, the sleigh had shuttled back and forth across the snow-covered ice, bringing in Kathleen and Tom, Ian and Edward, Dorothy and Don, Randee, John, Jason, Matt, Adam, and Brandy too. Brightly colored packages were piled high on the sleigh. The snowfield glittered in the sun. There was no wind to disturb the heavy, snow-laden branches of the great pines—just a deep and penetrating cold, which the dozens of active animals seemed not to notice.

Jeannie's family had brought supplies. The deer brought in their boxes on their backs, and the bears carried large sacks of food, carefully watched by the badgers to make sure the bears did not succumb to temptation and get into the supplies themselves.

That afternoon, Jeannie discussed plans for Christmas dinner with some of the older and wiser animals. They sat in a circle among the cedars on Molly Point. The group included one of the owls, Mr. Woodchuck, Belknap Beaver from Borden Lake, two of the deer, one bear, and Mr. O'Possum of Lynx Bay. Jeannie invited them and all the others to Christmas dinner at noon on Christmas Day. There was much discussion about the arrangements.

"We must have it outside," shouted Pudgey, who had slipped into the circle of animals from behind a large stump.

"Why not Watermelon Island?" suggested Mr. O'Possum.

"Too far," said Mr. Woodchuck.

"And besides," mused Belknap Beaver, "I believe North Crab Creek still has some open water around some of our family houses."

"Why not Lovers Island?" cried Jeannie. "It's perfect. There is the clearing among the great trees looking out over Lynx Bay and back toward Heller's Island. And there is plenty of room for dancing and entertainment and steep slopes down to the lake to keep the otters and bear cubs occupied for hours on end."

"Just the ticket," said Belknap. "We'll see to all the arrangements. We beavers know how to organize work."

The others all nodded their agreement, and Jeannie smiled as she thought of the enormous beaver dams and mud-retaining walls built in summer by the beavers up in Oxbow Creek. "Yes," she said to herself, "the beavers will have it all ready by tomorrow, Christmas Day."

That night, the families celebrated Christmas in the cottage around the big, stone fireplace. There were hot buttered rums and sweet mulled wine. There were turkey and stuffing, Christmas stockings, and many presents eagerly opened by all. Most of the animals went to bed early, but Pudgey and Mr. Woodchuck both came indoors to enjoy the proceedings. Jeannie held Pudgey on her knee, and Mr. Woodchuck stretched out on the floor near the fire. Before long, they were both asleep.

Jeannie covered both the old Mr. Woodchuck and Pudgey Bear with the tweed blankets used on the porch in the summer. Pudgey stirred, rolling over on his back and exposing his fuzzy tummy to the warm firelight. Jeannie stroked the soft fur and small paw of her little friend, who made soft growling sounds and fell deeper into his Christmas slumber.

Later, the lights winked off in the cottage, and the chimney smoke rose up through the trees where the owls continued their Christmas Eve watch, waiting for signs of St. Nick's sleigh passing across the northern lights.

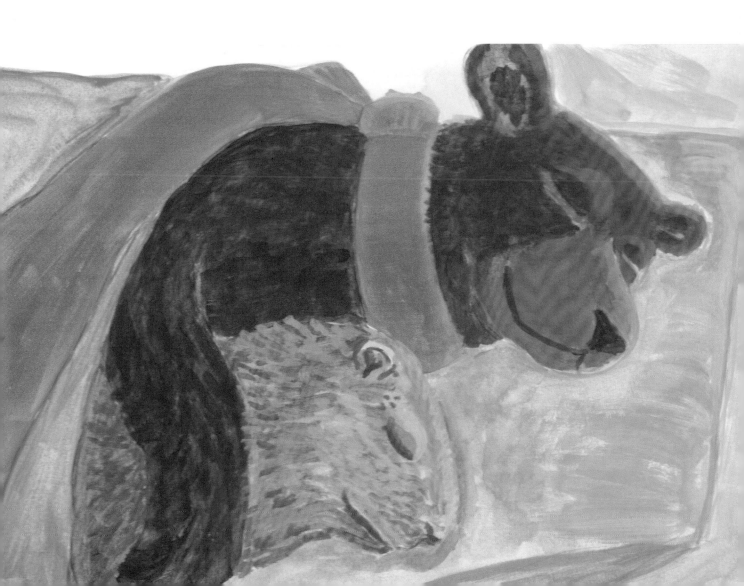

"Merry Christmas! Merry Christmas!"

High voices, low voices, smooth voices, gravelly, growling voices—all the animals shouted Christmas greetings all over the lake and through the woods. Bears growled it, cardinals sang it, beavers lisped it, and otters and squirrels chattered it.

Lovers Island was the center of activity. Boxes and bags, large and small, were carried there by all the animals. Bears pulled logs from the woods across the ice, and moles pulled individual walnuts over the snow on colored strings.

"Heave, ho!" shouted Boulder as he and his brothers pushed another box up the slope to the crest of Lovers Island.

"We are fixing the chutes," exclaimed the otters as they slid down the slopes with wet coats to make curved ice slides down the hill onto the lake.

"Wheeee!" shouted one of the little females as she slid like lightning down between the trees.

Pudgey tried the slide. "Yeow!" he screamed as he shot high in the air off a root bump at the shore. He got up, rubbing his bottom, and went back to work with the big bears.

Gradually, Lovers Island was transformed. A large fire was built at one end with a grate and sticks placed for cooking and heating pots of food and coffee. A large, round table of wood had been fashioned by the beavers overnight and was decorated with pine boughs, pinecones, birch bark, and bits of colored ribbon. Stumps and boughs were placed as seats, and there were stocks of blankets for the people to wrap up in to keep warm.

At noon, Jeannie called the clearing to order, and Christmas dinner began. Every animal and person had exactly what they wanted to eat. The tastes and scents were wonderful—many Jeannie had never experienced before. There was also much shouting, laughing, and rolling about in the snow.

Soon the entertainment began. The bears with their long scarves and brightly colored stocking caps pushed in close and sang the honey bear song:

"We are the honey bears
And we need honey!"

Jeannie caught a new refrain:

"We are the honey bears
And we need honey
And we need bear pop!"

Jeannie immediately provided the requested beverage, much to the delight of all the bears.

The deer did a stately ballet in the snow. The squirrels and otters put on the wild cancan dance they had performed the previous year, and the beavers held a tree-gnawing race to see who among them had the sharpest teeth and the strongest jaws.

Then the large crowd of families and their many animal friends settled down. Even the constant pushing and sliding of the otters and small bears down the slopes onto the lake came to a standstill. The older bears began to doze near the fire as the red winter sun settled on the treetops across the lake.

"This is Christmas Day," said Jeannie in her softest voice. The animals were all completely still now. "This is the world's most special day," she said, "and we are all here together, sharing our world and our lives."

Belknap, the old beaver, stood up and cleared his throat. "We are your friends. And you know how friendly we are in summer, even when we can't talk." He adjusted his gold spectacles and folded his hands across his stomach. "Every one of you is welcome in our home here in the woods at Crab Lake."

"Indeed," added Mr. Woodchuck.

"It is so," said all the others, led by Mr. O'Possum, who was now right in the middle of his own bay.

Belknap tapped his tail on the ground for attention. "On this Christmas Day, our Christmas gift to you is us—all of us—each and every one of us, and our great cathedral, the forest and the lake."

There was a long silence. Now the sun was down behind the trees. The sky was crimson with a few small, golden clouds. The light in the clearing of Lovers Island was a soft shade of mauve, and the deep green tops of the big Norway pines, flecked with snow, stood out against the pure, blue sky.

"Here in this place and among all of us," said Mr. Woodchuck, "there are no other gifts. None are needed, and some of the things people bring to us in summer are dangerous for us."

"It's the perfect Christmas," said Jeannie, her breath creating a frosty cloud in the evening air. "It is perfect because our gift is all God's creation, with all of us in it together, friends and families, animals and people, sharing our world. We need no other gifts."

And with this, Jeannie stood up and shouted, "Merry Christmas, everyone! Today and all days—summer, winter, spring, and fall!"

And the night gathered around the little group on Lovers Island. The fires burned brightly in the darkness and shed their dancing light across the snow.

And high above in the great pines, two bald eagles, proud and still, kept watch through the night over Jeannie and her sleeping family.

A Tale of Summer Freedom in the Wintertime

Winter came early to Crab Lake in 1991. Deep snow lay in the woods before the deer hunters could mount their campaign of terror against the animals. Bitter cold had closed the lakes by late October, and all of Jeannie's animal friends had by instinct prepared early for a long, cold winter.

By Christmas, many of Jeannie's best forest friends were already tired of winter. Snowy the snow owl hooted mournfully about the cold and lack of food. Quietly, he perched in the big hemlock next to the porch, swiveling his head all the way around, staring off into the woods. The deer awakened later than usual in the morning, spent more time nuzzling in the forest glens, and returned early to their hollows in the deep snow drifts as the reddening skies forewarned of gathering darkness. The burrowing animals and all their small friends spent hours in their underground dens, gathered round roaring fires, drinking birch-bark tea and swapping stories of summer adventures.

So when Jeannie came to Molly Point a few days before Christmas, all her friends were even more excited than usual. Pudgey was now a bigger bear, but he still acted like a cub—some said because he had been babied by Jeannie at a young and impressionable age. He always stood in front of Jeannie with his paws grasped together behind his back, his stocking hat askew over one ear, and his long scarf hanging over his tummy. He also still shuffled his right foot back and forth in the snow whenever he talked.

"It seems like February to us this year," he told Jeannie when she arrived. "At first, we played all day in the snow while the leaves were still on the trees. Then we took our winter naps, and when we woke up, winter was still here."

"That's right," echoed Boulder the Beaver. "We've been working in the snow and ice for months. I haven't had a good swim in open water for weeks and weeks."

"I am tired of winter too," said Mr. Woodchuck. "Now I just lie every day on the porch above the lake and wait to watch the sunset."

"But then after dark you go to Burrow Hall with all the small animals," complained one of the deer, "and drink tea with all the little folks while the rest of us stay out in the wind and the dark."

Then Jeannie heard the sage voice of Belknap Beaver, the old beaver from Borden Lake. He had walked over to Molly Point through the wooded trail from Baby Beaver Bay to pay his annual respects to Jeannie. "Really," he said. "It's a serious business. When the snow came, the eagles nearly didn't make it out in time to go south. And the loons finally had to take off in a blinding snowstorm with all of us assembled down on Molly Point, giving them encouragement for their long flight to Mexico."

Jeannie was concerned about this unusual drop in morale among her woodland friends. She started down the hill through the deep snow to the cedar tree that in summer marked the place for the pier. None of the animals cavorted in the snow or slid down the hill, but the old beaver walked by her side. "Frankly, Miss Jeannie, we've all been waiting for you this year even more than usual. We needed a little bit of a lift to get us through this extralong winter."

Jeannie sat on the shore where, in summer, the evening sun turned the mossy, needle-covered ground into a brilliant quilt of mottled green and brown and where each tree enjoyed its moment of glory in the otherwise darkening forest. She thought and thought of what to do, and Belknap sat beside her, making designs in the snow with his walking stick. Pudgey sidled down to the lake and sat like a lump in the snow, watching Jeannie with a long face and big, sad eyes.

"I have it!" Jeannie suddenly shouted, and she jumped up and grabbed Pudgey's cap off his head. "Where is the sleigh?" she cried, and the deer standing back in the trees looked around, alarmed that they had forgotten all about bringing the fancy Christmas sleigh.

A few minutes later, the sleigh was there—with four deer standing in harness and excusing themselves for being late.

"Please take me around the lake," said Jeannie. She jumped in the sleigh and said to Pudgey and Beaver, "Climb in here—I need your big voices."

Mr. O'Possum had been learning to drive the sleigh on her last visit. Now she saw him sitting there alone, his long, pink tail winding down from the back. "Good afternoon, madam," said Mr. O'Possum as he tipped his hat. "How nice to see you back at Crab Lake. Where shall we go?"

"Around the lake," cried Jeannie. "I have an announcement to make."

With that, the sleigh sped off across the snow-covered ice, making no sound and cutting two tracks in the otherwise undisturbed field of diamonds.

Jeannie gave instructions to Pudgey and Belknap, and soon they were shouting at the top of their voices:

"Come to Molly Point Tomorrow for an Adventure!

Heigh-ho, you there in the tree,
You in the hole,
You in the snow,
Come to the show,
Heigh-ho—heigh-ho!"

"Will there be honey?" Pudgey asked Jeannie hopefully.

"Yes," said Jeannie. "Honey and warmth and a wonderful story of summer."

The next day, out of the wind in the little bay behind Molly Point, the beavers brought wood for an enormous fire. All the animals came from the lakes around Crab Lake. There were animal delegations from Presque Isle, Horse Head, Armor, Annabelle, North Crab, South Crab, Van Vliet, Hurst, Borden, and even from Wolf, Bear, Round, and Clear Crooked. There was also a special group of frisky otters from Oxbow Creek and a work crew of beavers who said they were from Lac du Flambeau.

When all the animals had gathered around the warmth of the great bonfire and had their fill of hot soup, cocoa, birch-bark tea, honey, and boiled berries over angel cake, Jeannie climbed on top of a great stump that the bears had pulled out from the shore, and from this high position, she began to speak to the animals.

"I know you are tired of this extralong Northwoods winter. So today, I want to tell you a very special story about summer. This is a story about your kindred friends from all over the world, and it takes place in London, England, on a summer morning in June."

The animals looked at each other in expectation and settled deeper into the snow.

Jeannie continued, "There is a place in London called Regent's Park Zoo."

"What's a zoo?" burst out Pudgey.

"A zoo," replied Jeannie, "is a place where animals live in what is meant to be friendly captivity, so that people in the big cities can come and see them and learn about them. The animals come from all over the world, from the jungles of Asia, the bushland of Africa, the mountains and plains of Australia, from the Amazon in Brazil, from Russia, from Alaska, from America, and from the smallest islands of the Pacific. And all the animals live together in the zoo and are taken care of by a special group of people called zookeepers."

"Is it like Crab Lake?" asked Boulder.

"No," interrupted wise old Belknap. "It is not like Crab Lake. You are all lucky because you have never been to a zoo."

A nervous shudder spread among the animals. Everyone knew that Belknap Beaver was wise in the ways of the world. All the animals had seen him leaning against his beaver house in Borden Lake on lazy summer afternoons, reading large books through his thick glasses.

"Although zoo animals are well fed by their keepers and cared for in many ways," Jeannie explained, "they do not have their freedom, like each and every one of you."

The explanation was greeted with silence.

"Anyway," continued Jeannie, "one day in June, the zoo animals were asked to pack their bags and prepare to leave their cages. The head zookeeper explained that Regent's Park Zoo was to be closed temporarily for renovations, and all the animals were to prepare themselves for a long march to a new home. This, he said, was in a place called Whipsnade, deep in the English countryside.

"'Whipsnade? Whipsnade? What is Whipsnade?' The question spread that night through every cage in Regent's Park. There was great excitement among the lions and tigers, elephants, rhinos, zebras, gorillas, snakes, and all manner of smaller creatures that had gathered, according to instructions, outside their cages with cloth knapsacks and suitcases. A little after sunrise, the head zookeeper came striding down each row of cages, giving out instructions to the animals to assemble in the large grass field next to the zoo.

"'Elephants first!' he shouted. 'Zebras, bears, buffalos, and giraffes! Small animals, form parallel lines on either side of the big animals. Lions and tigers in the rear and rhinos and hippos at the very back!'"

At this point in Jeannie's story, she was forced to stop. Her friends at Crab Lake demanded to know what kinds of creatures she was talking about. Jeannie had brought pictures of all the zoo animals she spoke of, and when the Crab Lake animals saw them, they were amazed—amazed by the size, the color, and the diversity of this great band of animals that had formed themselves into a parade at Regent's Park.

"Soon, the great assemblage was ready to move," Jeannie continued. "The head zookeeper, seated high on one of the lead elephants, shouted instructions through his big red megaphone.

"'Let us begin the march to Whipsnade,' he shouted.

"The zoo animals shouted, 'TO WHIPSNADE, TO WHIPSNADE,' without having the least idea of what it was or where it was located. The zoo band struck up a march. All the animals stepped forward, and the zoo wagons creaked into motion. Soon the zoo animals had composed a chorus, which they repeated again and again:

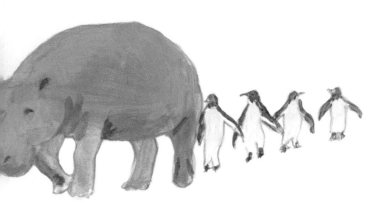

'Rumptee tiddelly
Rumptee too
Rumptee tiddelly
Rumptee too'

"They sang as they marched out of London and into the brilliant green of the English countryside.

Whipsnade
or
Bust

"At noon, the great procession stopped in a large meadow surrounded by stone walls, hedges, and tall trees. The head zookeeper announced a period of rest, and soon the animals broke free in total disorder. They climbed the walls, jumped over the hedges, climbed the trees, ran across the adjoining fields, dug holes, jumped in a nearby stream, and generally cavorted and played until the end of the day. The head zookeeper was only able to attract them back to the big field beside the running brook by laying out an enormous picnic. Soon the animals had eaten their fill and spread out, exhausted from their activities in the evening sunshine. The head zookeeper tried to rally the animals with his megaphone. Then he turned to the zoo band, but even the music failed to rouse the sleeping animals. Twilight descended, and the last slanting rays of the sun reflected on hundreds of sleeping animals dreaming dreams of freedom in the fields of England."

"Hurrah!" shouted Pudgey.

"Bravo," roared the bears.

"Capital," shouted the beavers, the otters, and the woodchuck.

"Wonderful," sighed the deer.

"Super," squeaked the mice, the chipmunks, the squirrels, and the moles.

"What happened next?" shouted Pudgey.

"Well," said Jeannie, "the next morning, when the zoo animals had awakened refreshed from their long slumber in the grass, the zookeeper asked them to reassemble, the band struck up, and, with a great deal of shuffling, roaring, coughing, scurrying, crawling, plodding, and pawing, the zoo animals once again assembled in a grand procession and began to march over the hills to Whipsnade. Their spirits were soaring, and again they chanted,

'Rumptee tiddelly

Rumptee too

Rumptee tiddelly

Rumptee too'

"At noon again, after just a few miles, the head zookeeper called a halt, and lunch was served in great barrels and troughs of food and water. The zoo animals ate and drank and then set off in all directions, refusing once again to reassemble into a procession. By evening, most of the animals came back for supper before settling down in their various groups to sleep under the midsummer stars.

"Every day for the next ten days, the march to Whipsnade followed the same pattern. The zoo animals arose at sunrise, assembled in the great procession, and marched through the morning to the rousing music of the zoo band. At noon, the animals insisted on their freedom for the rest of the day, and at night they gathered in the darkness to tell tales and to savor their day of freedom.

"People came from all over the South of England to watch this strange and wonderful sight. Banners had now been painted by the monkeys in bright colors and big letters: 'REGENT'S PARK ZOO ON THE MOVE' and 'WHIPSNADE OR BUST.'

"And so the wonderful days in the sun, crossing green hills, fording the streams, and cavorting in the fields and woods continued until, one day, they arrived at Whipsnade.

"But what was Whipsnade?" said Jeannie. "Another zoo—a nice zoo, a clean zoo, a country zoo—but, nevertheless, a zoo."

A groan swept through the Crab Lake crowd gathered on the ice behind Molly Point. It was cold now, but the big bonfire on the ice burned brightly. In the west across the lake, the sky was brilliant orange above the distant pines and birch trees.

"What does it mean?" cried Pudgey.

It was still but for the wind softly stirring the trees and the cracking sound of the great bonfire as the animals thought about the answer. The sky had turned a deep crimson, and the first stars appeared above the big hemlocks on the bay's eastern shore.

Then old Belknap came forward into the ring of dancing light from the bonfire. He climbed up onto the top of the stump next to Jeannie. Slowly, he put on his steel-rimmed spectacles with the extralong stems and fastened them carefully behind his small, furry ears. "Jeannie has told us a wonderful story," he said, his voice sounding deep and wise. The animals gathered round in the snow and listened without a sound.

"Jeannie has told us a story about our friends, brothers, and sisters from faraway lands who live their lives in captivity. She has told us about their days of freedom in the summer sun, running and jumping across the fields of England, swimming in the brooks and sleeping under the stars."

The animals listened, breathless, waiting for Belknap to continue. "But Jeannie also told us about ourselves. We are not zoo animals, living in cages, well fed and cared for by friendly people. Jeannie has reminded every one of us of our great good fortune. We are free, and we live in the wild—every day, every night, through all seasons, and in every kind of weather. In short, we are free . . . free forever!"

There was a moment of complete silence. Then Jeannie said, "Yes, my friends, you are free. At Crab Lake, you are free."

Suddenly all the animals were shouting at once. "We are free! We are free!"

"I'm Pudgey Bear—I'm free," cried Pudgey.

"Me too," cried Boulder.

"And me too," hooted Snowy the snow owl.

"Count me in," rasped Mr. O'Possum of Lynx Bay.

All the animals agreed, and Pudgey's voice rose in celebration. "It may be cold—"

"And dark," the otters cried together.

"And we may be short of food," giggled the deer.

"And honey too," laughed Pudgey.

"But we are Free, Free, Free,"

they all shouted in a great chorus.

"And summer *will* come again," finished Jeannie. "The snow will melt, the ice will break up, the trees will blossom, and life will begin again."

"Hurray!" roared the animals.

"Summer *will* come, and you will all be here. And so shall we—Jeannie, David, Kathleen, Tom, Randy, John, Jason, Matt, Adam, Ian, Edward, Dorothy, Don, and—and—KAITLIN JEANNIE!!"

"HURRAY FOR KAITLIN JEANNIE!" shouted all the animals, who were now dancing in the snow. "The cardinals from Phoenix passed us the news: Jeannie has a niece!"

The celebration continued long into the night. Sparks from the bonfire rose high into the frosty night air as the beavers threw on more logs. Dozens of Jeannie's friends came forward to thank her for the story of Whipsnade.

"Thank you for helping us through the winter," said a young doe through her thin, dark lips, "and thank you for reminding us of our freedom here at Crab Lake."

Later that night, the bonfire burned down to a warm, soft glow of reddish-orange coals; the smoke now rose in a column straight into the star-filled sky. Jeannie sat in the snow in a bright red blanket, watching the first streaks of dawn. The snow was trampled in all directions, and there were happy trails of footprints leading off in all directions—into the woods and across the wide and frozen expanse of Crab Lake.

Jeannie turned her eyes to the now brightening sky. Morning light touched a distant ridge of clouds, turning them a vivid pink against the violet of the western sky. She thought of freedom—then of winter, the long, cold nights, the short and often brilliant days—the animals living their lives in freedom. Then she saw the lake in summer with all her friends and the warm, breezy days on the dock. "Summer will come again—summer at Crab Lake. And we will all be free in the summer sun."

Escape of the Denver Polar Bear Cubs

In September 1995, the city of Denver went bankrupt. Denver's fabulous new airport had put the city over the edge. Public services and city projects were suddenly faced with disaster, and one of the first casualties was Denver's zoo.

In late October, the zoo was closed. City officials put the land up for sale, and Christie's of London came in to mount a huge auction of all the animals in the zoo. Day after dreary day, the gavel came down on the happy inhabitants of the Denver Zoo. The giraffes were sold to the National Zoo in Washington, DC; Denver's hippopotamus family went to the Munich Zoo; the baboons to a new home in New York, the lions to Phoenix, and the tigers to Regent's Park Zoo in London. Finally, Denver's two most popular attractions, Klondike and Snow, the polar bears born just eighteen months earlier and celebrated by the entire state of Colorado, were sold to the Toronto Zoo in Canada.

A few days later, on a frosty November morning, a gigantic crowd of Denver's devoted polar cub fans gathered at a small airport on the south side of Denver to see their beloved cubs off to their new home in Canada.

Thousands of waving children, many crying and clinging to their weeping parents, shouted goodbye.

The small aircraft revved its engines and plunged down the runway. In a few moments, it lifted upward, flying east into the deepening gray sky. The crowd dispersed reluctantly, but that afternoon, Denver came to a complete standstill when the news blared out, "Bear plane crashes! Klondike and Snow lost in plane crash"; "Polar Bear Mystery in Wisconsin!"

The small charter plane had crashed in a raging snowstorm on a frozen lake in northern Wisconsin. It had gone down in the darkness of early evening near a place called Manitowish Waters. The pilots had survived with minor injuries, saved by the deep snow, which had created a soft blanket over the broad surface of the frozen lake.

But the big news, the news that shocked the people of Denver, was about the bears. They were missing! Nowhere to be seen! Not a trace, not a sign! They had not gone through the ice, yet their tracks, if they had run away, were gone— obliterated by the wind and the swirling snow.

"Boy, is this fun!" shouted Klondike as he slid down a steep bank onto the icy surface of the lower Manitowish River.

Snow followed. "Wheee!" She collided with Klondike, who sprawled forward into an open hole in the ice.

"Hey, look!" exclaimed Klondike. "I got a fish." He held up his large paw to show Snow the trout he had captured almost by accident in the shallow water.

Soon Klondike and Snow were splashing about together, breaking the thin ice that lay above the surface of the fast water running along one edge of the small river. In a few minutes, they had caught and eaten a dozen fish—the freshest and most delicious fish they had ever tasted. They were fed and warm in their furry coats in the deep snow—intensely happy in the freedom of open space, nestling together against the rising north wind under the deepening red glow in the western sky.

The next morning, after a fish breakfast, Klondike and Snow set off through the woods along the high bank of the Manitowish River. Before long, the two white cubs struck the western end of Boulder Lake. They crossed the frozen bay and crashed through the woods to Clear Crooked Lake. They passed half-buried, deserted cottages. The roofs of the old log cabins seemed to sag under the weight of the snow, and small birds darted from cabin to cabin, nestling between the large logs.

The sun reflected a blinding brilliance off the vast, open snowfield covering Wolf Lake. They moved north, increasingly excited by their new freedom and by the beauty of the snow-clad lakes and forest. They found Bear Creek and followed its winding ice track to Round Lake. When they had crossed this lake and traversed its northern shoreline, they found no break or creek opening to the north. So they settled down to try breaking the ice in the shallows of the shoreline, romping and wrestling while they worked in the midday sun.

Suddenly, a small, clear voice broke the silence. "Who are you?" it said.

Klondike and Snow stopped and looked toward the wooded shoreline. "Why, you are all white!" it said again.

The voice came from a small black bear standing next to a tall Norway pine.

Klondike and Snow took a few steps toward the black bear. "We are polar bears. That's why we're all white," said the two cubs together. "Who are you?"

"Er-uh, I'm Pudgey Bear. I live at Crab Lake—which is that way," their new friend said. He pointed a fat, fuzzy paw with leathery pads on its underside toward the woods behind him. "I came over this morning across Little Beaver Bay and Borden Lake to eat fish in Bear Creek."

"We like to fish," exclaimed the polar cubs excitedly. "We fished yesterday for the first time."

"The first time?" Pudgey squinted in disbelief. He began shifting his weight from one paw to the other. Who were these strange white bears, he wondered? They were cubs still, but far from babies.

"Yes," explained Klondike. "Until yesterday, we lived in a zoo, and every day, two times a day, a man in a blue uniform came and fed us fish and biscuits."

Pudgey came forward out of the trees. He stood before Klondike and Snow and reached out to touch the cubs with a paw. "Er-uh, I am so sorry to hear you were in a zoo. At Crab Lake, we animals have only heard of zoos, but we know they are places where our brothers and sisters are held captive and have to stay all their lives in small cells with bars or fences." Tears welled up in Pudgey's big brown eyes and ran down his soft nose as his black paws rested on the pure-white fur of his new friends. "Welcome to Crab Lake!" he shouted. "Welcome to Crab Lake! Er-uh, er-uh—what are your names?"

"Klondike."

"Snow."

"We are the famous polar bear twins from Denver Zoo. *Everyone* knows us," the two cubs intoned in unison.

"Yes, we're famous; we've been on television," said Klondike, whose voice trailed off as he looked around the lake and saw the beauty of the snow-covered pines, standing straight and tall like so many regiments of soldiers stretching endlessly along the shore. "But we've noticed something new since we escaped yesterday," Klondike added, eyes wide. "We didn't know the world was *so big*."

"And so beautiful," sighed Snow.

"And so free," concluded Klondike.

"And so happy!" exclaimed Pudgey, who now began dancing about in the snow. "Crab Lake is a happy place; we're all happy here—all the time—summer and winter. And . . ." He paused. "—and . . . And we talk to our human friends here in winter . . . er-uh, not in summer . . . but-but we show ourselves in summer," Pudgey raced on. "Of course, mainly to our special friends."

The two polar cubs cocked their heads and looked at one another, listening intently to their new friend with the black, silky fur. "Our special friends are . . . Jeannie, and, er-uh, Kaitlin Jeannie—uh, David, Kathleen, Mr. Tom, and . . . and all their friends." Pudgey stopped, out of breath. "Belknap, the old beaver from Borden Lake, will tell you all about it. He knows everything." Pudgey puffed himself up with the pride he felt at his own very considerable knowledge. "But our best friend, our most beloved friend—and all the animals here agree—is Jeannie. Jeannie comes to see us every Christmas." Pudgey smiled his special bear smile and clapped his fat paws together. "Christmas on Crab Lake. That's what we call it when Jeannie comes. And you know what?" Pudgey winked at Klondike and Snow.

"What?" said the two white bears, now totally captivated by Pudgey.

"Christmas is coming soon."

And with this, all three bear cubs began celebrating by rolling in the snow together and shouting their excitement. The celebration went on until the three bears sat in the snow, exhausted. Then they scooped great paws of snow into their bright pink mouths to quench their thirst. In a few moments, they had caught their breath.

"Let's eat fish," shouted Pudgey, who made off toward the east shore, where the low brush marked Bear Creek. "Then we'll go to Crab Lake and get all the animals together to prepare Jeannie's Christmas surprise."

Klondike and Snow looked questioningly at Pudgey. "Surprise?"

"Polar bears at Crab Lake! Hooray!"

In the days that followed, the official search for Klondike and Snow went on throughout the Northwoods. Owners of lodges that stayed open in winter—such as Little Bohemia—were asked to keep an eye out for two young polar bears. Snowmobilers in Presque Isle and Boulder Junction were asked to keep a careful watch for polar bears.

But no sign of the bears was found. Back in Denver, the sadness over losing Klondike and Snow was gradually replaced by a quiet satisfaction, and then happiness, that two such popular white cubs were on the loose—free—in the Northwoods of Wisconsin.

"Godspeed to them," whispered one parent to another.

"Better than Toronto," said the old zoo workers.

"Now they are free in their own home," said the children.

Even the Denver TV reporters who had made Klondike and Snow famous settled down to make up programs about the cubs' new life in the wild.

After a few weeks, even the Wisconsin forest rangers stopped looking for Klondike and Snow. "Go free, my friends," they murmured over morning coffee with the loggers at the Outdoorsmen.

"Besides, it's nearly Christmas," said one of the loggers. "What greater gift than freedom?"

"You bet," said one ranger. "You got that right."

Now the days reached their shortest time. The sun rose in midmorning and set red streaked in the western sky by midafternoon. The snow cover grew deeper. On windy days, the snow drifted, and the bare trees roared in their winter slumber. On bright days, the snow sparkled like millions of diamonds, and the animals laid tracks through the forest and across the lakes. Sometimes the cold was so intense, so still, that one could hear the flutter of a wing or the snapping of a twig high in the great trees.

At night the animals rested, waited, in their burrows, in their houses and nests, in their snow holes, keeping warm, watching, sensing the shift toward spring, which still lay weeks ahead.

In the sleeping wintertime forests of Wisconsin, Klondike and Snow learned about freedom and nature. They were taught by Belknap the beaver to listen to all the sounds; they learned from the deer how to be swift; the bears taught them how to make fish holes in the ice; the red fox taught them caution and woodcraft; the owls stressed patience, the beavers industry, and the otters the pure joy of fun and freedom. Klondike and Snow learned how to sniff the wind for scents of weather or danger. They recovered their natural instincts from the deep past and began to see themselves as bears, polar bears, free bears—rather than as famous bears.

The bear cubs who blended so perfectly with the snow and the birch trees were reborn at Crab Lake, discovered their roots in nature, and came home—like so many of those who stand as they did among the cedars on Molly Point.

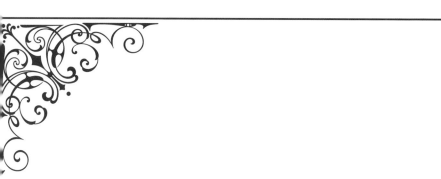

Two days after the shortest day of the year, Klondike and Snow were asked to take their place at the end of a long line of animals formed all along the entry road to Molly Point. All the animals from Crab Lake were there. The deer stamped the snow and nibbled on the lower limbs of the cedar trees. The bears sat sleepily on the ground, their time for a long winter's nap rapidly approaching. Beavers stood in small groups, talking and working away on various small carving jobs. Badger, the porcupine family, the weasels, rabbits, squirrels, and all manners of small animals were on hand. Above were the birds, many of them brilliant red cardinals, chirping expectantly about the approach of Christmas.

Down at the end of the road by the cottage stood the entire O'Possum family of Lynx Bay, except Mr. O'Possum, all dressed this year in pink jackets with slits cut for their long, gray tails, which curved down onto the snow.

"What are we waiting for?" Klondike asked the old woodchuck with the long, gray whiskers.

"Why, my dear polar bear," said Mr. Woodchuck, "we are waiting for Jeannie, who is coming today from England."

"Yes, home of my ancestors—so well portrayed in *Wind in the Willows*," a large brown rat chimed in. He had a long, pointed nose and was dressed entirely in orange-and-red wool tartan, complete with cap and scarf. "In those days," sighed Rat, "the toads had real class—up there at Toad Hall and all. These poor toads—up in North Crab and Ox Bow Creek, not to mention the fellows back in Jeannie's glen—they're not in the same league as Mr. Toad of Toad Hall. From what Jeannie read to us last Christmas, he was a noble toad, a toad of weightiness—"

"—though not discretion," cut in Belknap, the old beaver from Borden Lake. "You should watch what you say about the toads, Rat. They are asleep now and cannot defend themselves . . . and you're happy enough to play with them in summer."

"Where are my friends the moles?" said Rat, changing the subject. "You know, I'm very close to the moles," he added to the polar bears. "Fine fellows, one and all."

"Well," said Belknap, taking out his steel-rimmed spectacles and placing them behind his ears. "Molly Mole and all her family are tucked in the back of the sleigh with Jeannie. Others are in their dens under the hemlocks down by the Point, looking after the small animals. And our newest friend, Starnose of Papoose Lake, is in the cottage helping to put decorative frosting on Kaitlin's special Christmas cake. You are aware, I am sure, Rat, of the superb designs Starnose can produce with his nose, while the rest of us have such difficulties with our paws."

The old beaver paused in reflection. The polar bears had been listening with rapt attention and wide brown eyes. "You'll remember—you, Rat, and Boulder, and you, Pudgey—how, last summer, Jeannie saved Starnose's life over on Papoose Road." Belknap blinked, adjusted his large, flat tail, and puffed his fur against the cold. "Starnose has not forgotten and, in fact, this fall personally constructed a great labyrinth of tunnels down on the slope to Jeannie's breakfast dock."

Belknap Beaver cleared his throat and continued in his slow, measured voice, carefully and perfectly pronouncing each syllable of every word. "Starnose says that this summer Jeannie (and Kaitlin) will be able to watch dozens of their mole friends move about and carry out their daily duties while she has breakfast in the morning sun in a sort of mole laboratory on the hillside."

The polar bears had been carefully instructed by Pudgey to stand at the end of the line, off to one side by the new birch trees, close by where Jeannie's sleigh would come to a stop. Pudgey now came up to give final instructions.

"Do you think we'll recognize Jeannie from her visit to Denver Zoo?" Snow asked.

"Well, *she* never forgets an animal friend, and all of us remember when *we* first saw Jeannie."

"And what about Kaitlin?" they asked. "We know she likes bears because she placed a brick with her name on it at Phoenix Zoo to help the animals."

Suddenly, the snowy owl flew into the clearing with a great flapping of wings. He was as pure white as the two polar bears, with handsome yellow eyes as bright as the afternoon sun.

"To-whoo, to-whoo, to whom it may concern," came the owl's scholarly voice. "Whooray, who, who, whooray—Jeannie's on her way! They're just crossing the continental divide at the old portage to South Crab. Who, who, who, who."

Jeannie was less than a mile away, and the magic sleigh would be coming fast. Soon, they heard its bells, just over the hill beside the swamp where the cattails stood.

Now the animals could see the sleigh, cresting the hill between the big white pine and the boxwood tree. Clouds of moisture burst into the cold air with each deep breath of the deer pulling the sleigh. Mr. O'Possum had taken over as driver, and he was resplendent in his pink coat and gray top hat. Small fry—squirrels, chipmunks, mink, and one fox—jumped off the sleigh while it was still moving and rolled in the snow among their friends, who were now loudly cheering.

Then the sleigh came to a stop. Inside, tucked snugly beneath the heavy quilts and bright red blankets, surrounded by luggage and brightly wrapped Christmas boxes, were Jeannie and Kaitlin. The deer stood in their bright red harnesses, pawing the snow, panting, and tossing their beautiful heads. Clouds of steam rose in the bitter cold from their sleek brown bodies.

Mr. O'Possum laid the reins to one side and, turning to Jeannie and Kaitlin, announced in his most cultured voice, "Ladies, I am pleased to say that we have arrived at Molly Point, Crab Lake, in the great state of Wisconsin."

"Hooray!" cried the great throng of animals. "Welcome, Jeannie! Welcome, Kaitlin! Welcome to Crab Lake, and Merry Christmas!"

There was a moment of silence as Jeannie and Kaitlin climbed out from under the blankets and quilts. Mr. O'Possum of Lynx Bay, now down from the high driver's seat, opened the shiny red door of the sleigh and helped Kaitlin down the step. She stood, bundled up in her new pink Bon Point snowsuit with the long, red scarf and tall, red boots. Kaitlin was now four and a half years old, and although she talked and talked and talked about everything under the sun and very often danced for hours on end, she now stood stock still—amazed—by this very large group of talking animals.

The animals turned shy. They coughed and shuffled about in the snow, some pushing others forward from behind. Many had Christmas hats and bright scarves, some wore jackets, and others—the older animals—had cubs, pulling their little ones on sleds.

But if Kaitlin was surprised by all her new friends and the animals made shy by the little girl in the pink snowsuit, Jeannie was astounded and astonished when her eyes fell on the two polar bears.

"Why, what is this? Can it be . . ."

Pudgey stepped forward. "Er-uh-er-uh, I'd like to introduce our two new friends, Klondike and Snow."

"Klondike! Snow!" exclaimed Jeannie. "We thought you were lost in the woods. What a surprise! What a wonderful surprise!"

"Yes!" shouted Pudgey, now beside himself, hopping about sideways in the snow. "They are from Denver! They were in a zoo there and were fed fish twice every day by a man in a blue uniform, and, er-uh, they are famous and were even on television, and, and—"

"And now we're here at Crab Lake!" squealed the white cubs.

"Where we want to stay!" shouted Klondike.

"To live with all our friends and be free," added Snow.

"We love it here at the lake!"

"Yes, just as we do!" shouted Kaitlin. "Especially at Christmas—when the animals all talk."

The animals were now no longer shy. They rushed forward, carrying the bear cubs, Kaitlin, and Jeannie through the deep snowdrifts, down the hill, and on to the lake. There, they danced and wrestled about until the shadows deepened and the sky turned a soft pink and orange.

The lights now showed soft and golden in the cottage windows. Smoke rose from the stone chimney into the darkening sky. It was clear and very cold. Soon, the stars were out, forming a milky canopy in the clear sky with several brilliant gems sparkling near the low horizon.

Inside the cottage, Jeannie met more friends. Starnose was on the counter, charcoal brown and fuzzy, finishing the top of Kaitlin's cake. Big Guy was in one of the soft chairs over by the fire, sleepy from having been awakened earlier in the day by Boulder up in North Crab Creek. The red fox family had put up decorations, some cut and polished by the beavers. A fire burned softly in the stone fireplace.

All the animals were invited in for a special show. Kaitlin was the star of the show, dressed now in her special yellow costume, dancing "Chicken Chow Mein." The large animals, such as the deer and big bears, had to stand on the porch or look through the windows, but all the smaller animals were inside.

Jeannie stood before the large crowd, in which there was a good deal of fidgeting and jostling. "This is a special Christmas," said Jeannie. "We are so thankful that Klondike and Snow are here tonight."

"Hooray! Hooray!" shouted the animals together.

"And so happy that they will live at Crab Lake."

"Welcome to Crab Lake!" shouted Pudgey.

Klondike and Snow had been given seats of honor next to Jeannie and Kaitlin. They sat over by the doors to the porch, which were open so the large animals could hear and the polar bears didn't get too warm.

Pudgey had climbed the stairs behind the stone chimney and stood on the small balcony overlooking the large cathedral living room. He tapped the log railing and began leading the animals in shouting out a song:

"Polar bears at Crab Lake!
Crab Lake Christmas!
Polar bears at Crab Lake!
Crab Lake Christmas!

One, two, three, four
Jeannie loves polar bears
Four, three, two, one
Kaitlin loves the little ones

Hooray, hooray, hooray!
Polar bears are here to stay!"

Klondike and Snow bowed to their new friends. Klondike lifted Kaitlin onto his shoulders, and Jeannie raised her hands for silence. "Tonight is Christmas, and we are at Crab Lake. This is a white Christmas"—there was cheering from the animals—"but these special cubs of Christmas cheer will stay white all the year!"

Jason Builds a New Molly Point Log Cabin

The summer of 2000 at Crab Lake was no different from previous summers. In late May, the caretaker from Presque Isle came to Molly Point to put the docks into their usual places along the lakeside shore and in the back bay. George and Martha, the two bald eagles who came to Crab Lake every summer, arrived in April when the ice was breaking up on the lake. By the end of June, the steady shrieking of the new brown eaglet in the nest at the top of the ancient white pine on Judd's Point could be heard from daybreak to sunset.

In the woods up near the cabin, the foxgloves were spread along the edge of the path to the lake and back through the small clearings along the driveway. Forget-me-nots were thick on the ground behind the cottage. In July, white daisies and black-eyed Susans joined them on the sunny slope outside the back door.

Once again, Jeannie and David enjoyed the long, lazy days on Molly Point. There were breakfasts in the peaceful seclusion of the back bay, watching the ducks and dozens of dragonflies flit about over the water, and afternoons in the sunshine on the front dock, with canoeing expeditions to North Crab or Baby Beaver Bay over the old portage. Each day, two loons came fishing in the sunshine by the dock and later, at sunset, played loudly with a larger circle of their loon friends out in the center of the lake.

The summer days lengthened. Summer storms came up suddenly across the lake from the west—violent winds swept into the calm before the storm, pushing the startled lake before the rain, the lightning, and the deafening thunder. Then it was August, and spots of color appeared in the trees, sunsets came earlier, and there was an unforgiving chill in the air for the morning dip.

This was how Jeannie had always known Crab Lake in summer, and yet there was to be a change at Molly Point, and it worried Jeannie all summer long. One day, she brought it up to Kaitlin when the family all went for Kaitlin's Day on the island that bore her name. Here in the peaceful clearing, so well concealed from anyone on the lake, and with tea brewing in the fisherman's teakettle, Jeannie expressed her growing fears.

"You know, Kaitlin, just after Labor Day, we will begin building the new cottage."

"Yes, and it's great!" enthused Jeannie's niece. "I can hardly wait. Will I get to choose my own room?"

"I want the big bedroom downstairs with its own fireplace," Kathleen interjected.

"I want to face the lake," Kaitlin added.

"What about me?" asked Dorothy. "Where shall I be? I might like the other downstairs room, with the patio going out above the lake."

"You might like your own room, Kaitlin," suggested Jeannie. "Upstairs, snug behind the big fireplace chimney, where you can hear all the sounds of the woods at night and the rain on stormy evenings beating on the roof. But first, we have to build the new house. And that's my worry."

"Why?" asked Kathleen. "The plans are all set—the builders come in two weeks."

"That's just it!" wailed Jeannie. "What's to be done about the animals? They're not ready for all the noise and disruption! It will go on all winter and into next spring!" Jeannie looked around at her family circled on the big quilt. "Don't you see? Their peace and security will be destroyed. They will be frightened when the big trees are cut down and the earth is torn open. Some of our smaller friends, like the moles, the squirrels, and the woodchucks, may lose their homes and be forced to flee!"

Jeannie paused, visibly gasping for breath, her eyes showing the depth of her concerns. Now all the family was silent, staring at Jeannie. They all knew that Jeannie shared an extraordinary bond with nature. Everyone understood. Why else would the animals talk to Jeannie, or show themselves so freely? Be so friendly and trusting in so many other ways?

"The animals will fear that a great catastrophe is taking place," Jeannie said, "and this will happen long before they see the new cabin take shape and us living in it as we do the old cottage." She paused again. There were tears on her cheeks. "And with the new logs going up and the old cottage completely gutted, there'll be no Christmas at Crab Lake this year. The animals will think we've deserted them."

Jeannie looked at David now. "We can't just round them up next summer. What if we can't find them—they disappear—because they are frightened of what they see and hear at Molly Point? Hammers, saws, bulldozers, cranes, and strange men—the kind who hunt deer and geese in the fall!" Jeannie looked around the circle. "The animals know, and they'll probably go deep into the forests around Bear Lake—and then, there will be no one to wake Big Guy, the old turtle who hibernates under the ice in North Crab Creek, and he and everyone else will miss Christmas!"

"The only solution," said David, intervening quietly in the failing light, "is to make a call on old Belknap Beaver over at Borden Lake. We'll canoe over there toward sunset tomorrow and see if he'll come out to see you. Remember, he said what to do if you ever needed him—and it's already worked once."

And that settled the matter. The canoes were loaded in the shallow water among the reeds, and soon the family was paddling back to Molly Point. In the western sky was the brilliant orange afterglow of sunset, and over the still lake, broken only by the paddle's even strokes, came the sounds of the woods settling down for the night.

The next day it rained. But in the afternoon, it cleared, and the woods sparkled in the lowering rays of the late afternoon sun. "This is the perfect time to find Belknap," observed David. "The sun will set clear, and it will be a good night with a full moon for the beavers to really go to work."

Jeannie and David eased the *Jeannie* into the water and paddled south along the eastern shore of Crab Lake, past Echo Bay, the Countryman's, Sunset Point, and finally into the old portage bay. Soon they were gliding out from the Beaver Pond into the perfect stillness and buttery afternoon light of South Crab.

Here was a lake where man had never lived. Its shoreline of brilliant green grasses, white birch trees, moss-covered logs, and large granite rocks was perfectly reflected in the glass-like surface of the lake, with a depth and hue more startling than the shoreline itself. South Crab's perennial loon couple with their fuzzy babies, floating nearby, gave no signs of concern at the approaching canoe. A deer, roused from his afternoon nap near the shore, plunged noisily through the thick birch forest, coughing his displeasure at being wakened. Above, one of the eagles circled over the treetops. Nothing else stirred, and the paddles dipped noiselessly in the still water.

After crossing Baby Beaver Bay, Jeannie and David left the canoe and climbed up the ridge to Borden Lake. Jeannie had her canoe paddle, as Belknap had instructed those many years ago, and with David she sat to wait for the deep, rich light of sunset.

At dusk, Jeannie stood up and smacked her paddle three times on the surface of the shallow water. Each time, there was a loud crack that echoed back from the darkening shadows at the end of the lake.

Something stirred the surface down to the right, not far from the first beaver house. Ripples appeared, forming a *V* on the dark surface, and at the point of the *V*, Jeannie could make out the large, furry head of her most trusted friend, old Belknap the beaver of Borden Lake.

In a few moments, he emerged on the shore and stood facing Jeannie, propped up by his heavy, flat tail. Belknap did not make a sound; no word could be spoken in summer, but he was fully attentive. As if to prove it, the old beaver took his spectacles out from his fur pocket, placed them on his nose, and hooked the long stems carefully over his little ears, which were set well back on his large head.

"Oh, Belknap, I'm so glad to see you," said Jeannie, wringing her hands. "Thank you so much for coming."

Belknap didn't stir. Water dripped softly from his thick, wet fur. "We have a problem with Christmas this year," Jeannie said. She proceeded to tell Belknap the whole story: all her fears for the animals, the disruption at the construction site, the felling of the big trees, her fears for the burrows of the small folk who in a few weeks would need to be in their dens preparing for winter.

"And of course, Christmas," she concluded. "There can be no question of Christmas at Crab Lake this year."

Jeannie stopped. What had happened? There stood Belknap, just as before, but now his head was tipped to one side, as if he were puzzled.

Jeannie turned to David. "Why does Belknap look puzzled?" she asked. "He's never done that before."

Then, suddenly, another strange thing happened. In the wink of an eye, a brilliant red cardinal landed on Belknap's right shoulder, nodded at Jeannie, and then sang a most beautiful song—the very same song Jeannie and David had heard the cardinals sing in Virginia on days of the brightest sunshine and the softest of breezes high in the tops of the big trees.

What was he saying? Jeannie's thoughts raced ahead. The cardinals were friends, messengers, gossips: they could move a piece of news faster than the wires—anywhere in the world.

"That's it!" she shouted. "We have news! And the cardinals will spread it far and wide."

"And what's the news?" inquired David, perplexed.

"Why, the news is from Belknap—and it's a question. That's why his head is cocked over to one side and he asked the red cardinal to come to his shoulder. Don't you see?"

"Well—maybe," said David. "But I think there's more to Belknap's message. He's telling us that the cardinals will spread the news of what's happening. He's asking why we will not hold Christmas at Crab Lake this year. After the animals are told what is happening and the curious animals see the half-up cottage, seeing us at Christmas will help them understand."

"So we have to put on Christmas at Crab Lake no matter what," Jeannie concluded. "If we come here to reassure them, our friends' fears will all be forgotten. Belknap is right. We must have Christmas at Crab Lake, and the cardinals will spread the message."

Jeannie turned back to Belknap, but he was gone, and so was the cardinal. Out on the lake where it was almost dark, Jeannie's eye caught the line of ripples, and just beyond, she could see the large old head. She looked down, humbled by the simple wisdom of her friend. And there, almost touching her moccasin, was a bright red feather left by the cardinal— perhaps a promise of Christmas at Crab Lake.

The roar of diesel engines and the grinding of steel on steel early one September morning shattered the indian summer stillness of Crab Lake. Within the hour, a huge hemlock and several sturdy birch trees had been cut down. A bright yellow CAT, beeping endlessly every time it reversed, was clearing small trees and brush, levelling the ground around the building site. A large backhoe set to work digging a deep hole just behind the old cottage, and freshly loaded dump trucks labored noisily up the dirt track that served as driveway into Molly Point.

In the next days, several pickup trucks appeared, and men in flannel shirts, work pants, brimmed caps, and big boots crawled over the rugged desolation that used to be the woods just behind the old cottage. Now the old cottage looked small, naked, and utterly forlorn. Behind the cedar logs of the old house, Jason Roberts could be heard cracking and banging as he tore out its familiar insides.

Within days, the cement trucks had invaded the site to pour the concrete basement. It rained, producing a veritable quagmire of mud. Trucks got stuck, and a bulldozer pulled them out of the mire. All was noise, confusion, mud, and slime.

Gut the animals had long abandoned the scene of "the attack," as it was called. Several mole families and any number of mice, squirrels, and woodchucks had found new shelter in the roots and other accommodations down near the lake. Dozens of house mice from the old cottage were camped out with their country cousins. Other small animals had brought food and blankets to their uprooted friends and helped them make preparations for winter, which could begin with an early snowfall any day. At night, the bears and beavers helped move logs and branches, and Mr. O'Possum of Lynx Bay and all the little O'Possums pitched in to help their friends.

"A terrible business," proclaimed Pudgey Bear as he surveyed the scene of devastation.

"T-whoo, t-whoo, what's to do? What's to do?" the owls intoned at night in the trees above the site.

"We must be careful as can be with these men about," cautioned Boulder Beaver.

George the eagle overheard these comments from high in a nearby Norway pine. The intimidating champion of the lake had not yet started south for the winter, and he flapped his wings and snapped his large, yellow beak. "Yes, care and caution are in order," he said. "But above all, be brave and believe—remember the message the cardinals brought from Jeannie. All will be well at Molly Point, and there will be Christmas at Crab Lake."

"Hooray!" shouted the ring of animals gathered around the gaping hole in the earth. "Hooray for Jeannie!"

The first snow came early in the fall of 2000, just enough to cover the raw building site in a clean, white blanket. The snow did not stop the workmen, who came each day at daylight and worked until dark. At night, Boulder Beaver and Pudgey Bear prowled around the site. Owlie and Owlette kept watch from distant treetops and listened with their supersensitive ears for early morning sounds of approaching workmen. Near dawn, several foxes took over the watch. The animals agreed that the deer should stay far away during the hunting season. The foxes were by far the best suited to watch from the woods near the site and escape quickly if they were discovered.

Each evening, the foxes traversed the forest paths around Baby Beaver Bay, through the swamps around Bear and Wolf Lakes to Clear Crooked. Here, the animals gathered around a large fire and heard the day's news from the foxes and the owls.

After Halloween, they heard a tale of monstrous trucks, longer and higher than anything ever seen before, powering through the snow on South Crab Road. With their headlights beaming into the forest as they crested each hill in the road and their tall, silver stacks breathing dark, acrid fumes, these monsters made a frightening impression on the animals, spread out in hiding along the road. Their trailers were covered in bright blue tarps, so the animals had no idea what the trucks were bringing to Molly Point.

Then, one night, the foxes reported that there were logs, large, white logs, logs larger than any seen at Crab Lake, logs of all lengths, stacked in piles around the new hole in the ground.

That same night, the animals, including the deer, ventured through the woods to Molly Point. The deer sniffed at the logs. The bears, porcupines, squirrels, and many others climbed over the piles. But it was the beavers who examined the logs with the eyes of true engineers. They discovered that the ends had been shaved off straight and smooth. They noticed that the logs were huge trees and that all the bark had been removed. And, most importantly, they observed the large notches cut near the ends of each log.

"These are made to be put together!" exclaimed Boulder Beaver.

"We'd better see about these for our dams and houses," observed old Belknap, who had made the trek with the other animals. "Then our dams would stay in the rivers for good, and we could build more."

Before dawn, it began to snow. Suddenly, the animals heard the warning of the owls that workmen were approaching, and they scattered in all directions. Most were too curious to go very far, and so that day, the day the men began putting logs up with a crane to form walls, most of the animals were watching from the safety of the woods.

Although still frightened by the machines and men and uncertain why the old house had to go, the animals were satisfied to see the new cabin forming. "An old and new home," Belknap said, removing his spectacles. "A place for Jeannie and all of us."

The workmen that day were baffled. "Who made all these hundreds of tracks in the snow?" asked the foreman. "Every animal under the sun was here last night."

The workmen looked around, scratching their heads, and saw only the silent woods. But Jason knew who had made the tracks, and he would tell Jeannie that very night.

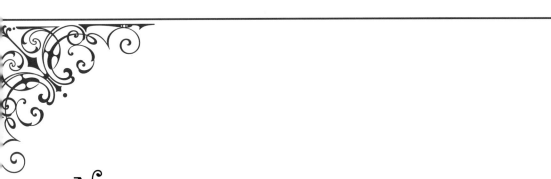

$\mathcal{N}$ow the animals ventured from their hidden lookouts in the woods each night to inspect progress on the new house and the old cottage. Jason and the workmen saw the telltale signs of their visits whenever there was fresh snow.

In December, the bitter cold arrived. In a matter of days, Crab Lake was frozen over. At night, the northwest wind would roar through the big pines and naked trees, bringing with it driving snow that drifted deeper and deeper on the road and over the building site.

Still the work went on. The animals celebrated the completion of the roof, and then a big truck with chains on its tires and some help up the hill from a bulldozer brought the windows. A few days before Christmas, the windows were in place, and smoke from the chimney signaled the first fires in the new house.

Two days before Christmas, the work stopped. Only Jason turned up with three others to work in the old cottage. That night, while the animals were circling the log house, unable to find a way to get inside, they suddenly heard the warning hoot of the owls. A few minutes later, they heard the sound of sleigh bells, and, looking out through the trees, they saw lights moving across the ice on the lake.

As the lights came closer, the animals could see that they were lanterns, lanterns on a sleigh—the magic sleigh of years gone by. Pulling the sleigh were two of the largest deer, and high on the driver's seat in his pink tails and tall silk hat sat Mr. O'Possum of Lynx Bay.

Up the path from Molly Point came the jingling sleigh, and the animals noticed it was piled high with Christmas packages, on the tallest of which were perched two bright red cardinals. The sleigh came to a stop before the front door of the new log house. The animals closed quickly around the sleigh, and Pudgey Bear stepped forward into the circle of light cast from the lanterns. He peered up into the sleigh and saw the familiar face of his friend, Jeannie, in a white fur hat.

"Hooray!" shouted Pudgey. "Hooray! Jeannie's here for Christmas!"

All the animals shouted together, "Hooray! Hooray! Hooray!" and began cavorting in the snow.

Jeannie stepped down from the sleigh, holding in her arms a bright red blanket. Inside, looking out at his friends, was Big Guy!

"We stopped in North Crab, found the string in the ice, cut a hole, and woke Big Guy up for Christmas," she said happily.

"Hooray for Big Guy!" the animals shouted. They knew now it really was Christmas.

"Come inside," cried Jeannie. "We have to build fires."

"And to decorate for Christmas!" shouted Pudgey.

Jeannie opened the door, and the animals streamed inside, looking about at the empty cabin and up to the tops of the huge log walls and roof. The cardinals perched on one of crossbeams.

Belknap walked in the door then. "Welcome, Jeannie. Welcome to our new home and to Crab Lake for Christmas."

A Gift in a Snowstorm

The big red snowmobile crested the last hill and came to an abrupt stop. The two riders, Jeannie and David, let the quiet of the forest gather around them as they looked down on Molly Point. Nothing stirred in the fading afternoon light—no birds, no breeze to loosen snow from the boughs of the big hemlocks—and no animals were there to greet them.

Molly Point Cabin with its deep brown logs and snow-covered roof lay nestled in the snow. Behind the cabin, down the hill toward the point itself, Jeannie and David could see through the big trees the broad expanse of snow that covered Crab Lake. The cabin was in darkness. Its stone chimney showed no sign of life; no comforting woodsmoke rose into the cold air. Huge icicles hung from the corners of the roof, but there were no sparkling lights to tell of the coming of Christmas—now just days away. Only one spot of bright color caught their eye as they surveyed the stillness of the scene before them. On its post over the snow-covered deck, the red standing out against the canopy of pines, was America's flag, in its place year round, night and day, in all seasons.

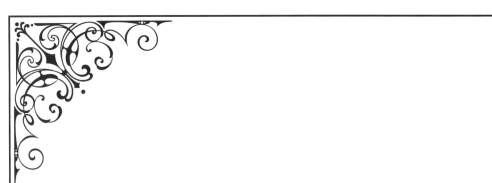

Jeannie thought of all that had happened here in the first year of the new century. She recalled the beginning of a great project when the sights and sounds of construction had rent the peace and silence of the woods. She remembered the earth being torn open, the trees being felled, her terrified woodland friends running for cover.

When the cabin was being built, Jeannie had nearly despaired of the damage to the forest and the fear struck into her Crab Lake friends. Many of the smaller animals, such as the woodchucks, the squirrels, the moles, and the rabbits, had been forced to move due to the construction.

Fortunately, Jeannie had been able to warn her old friend, Belknap the beaver, of the upcoming changes. Although he could not talk in summer, he had been able to listen, and he had spread the word about the new cabin to the other animals and had reassured them that there would be Christmas at Crab Lake after all. The animals had faithfully kept watch for weeks as the log walls went up and the roof went on.

All the animals had gathered last Christmas Eve in the shell of the new house, closed in from the cold and in front of a roaring fire. Jeannie had promised them all—Pudgey Bear, the deer, Owlie and Owlette, Big Guy, the moles, woodchucks, Boulder Beaver and his workmates, the otters, the eagles, and all the O'Possum family of Lynx Bay—that in summer the new house would be finished. Quiet and solitude would return to Molly Point, the men and machines would leave, the ugly gashes in the soft earth would be healed, and next Christmas—Christmas of 2001—would be a real family Christmas at Crab Lake for everyone.

Now it was nearly dark. A few stars were visible in the twilight, and the thin slice of a new moon had risen above the tamaracks in the swamp behind the log garage. How long had they stood there on the hill? The snow was sparkling now in the soft light of the stars and the moon. Jeannie and David broke a track in the snow where there was nothing but a smooth, unbroken surface of white.

$\mathcal{E}$arly the next morning, it began snowing. At first, the snow was light and fine, but by midmorning, the wind had come up from the north, sweeping across the frozen lake, swirling the snow around the cabin and through the trees. That whole day, the wind roared steadily in the treetops. Jeannie's animal friends were nowhere to be seen.

"They must be in their dens and burrows," Jeannie mused. "They know this is a big storm."

Jeannie was right. The moles were snug in their elaborate tunnels under snow and tree roots beside the lakeshore. The beavers had disappeared into their homes, skimming under the ice and climbing up onto the various shelves inside their houses. The deer had retired deep into the woods, where they could shelter under the snow banks in deep ravines or in the thick groves of young hemlock and spruce trees.

Large, fluffy snowflakes fell in what seemed an endless cascade, muffling all sound except their own delicate contact with the ground and trees. Inside the cabin, fires snapped and crackled in every fireplace as Jeannie and David, Jason, Jodie, Jacob, and Justin prepared the house for Christmas. They brought in fresh pine boughs from the woods to spread across each fireplace mantle and icicle lights to hang outside along the edge of the roof around the stone chimneys and along the deck railings. Armloads of firewood arrived, brought through the snow by faithful forest friends and carried into the house by Jason and David. Smells of baking and spices wafted through every part of the house.

Still it snowed. Still no animal friends appeared. But as the snow continued, Jeannie began to worry—would the rest of her family be able to get to Crab Lake?

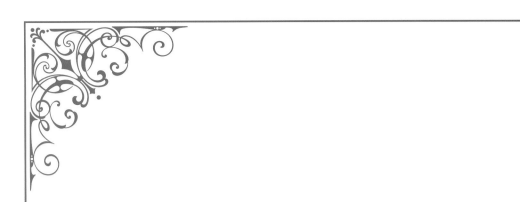

$\mathcal{A}$t sunset, the snow stopped. The temperature fell to zero, too cold for snow. Brilliant crimson clouds filled the western sky, turning the whole of Crab Lake's snowy surface pink. It was December 21, the first day of winter.

As the color faded and darkness moved out from the forest, Jeannie heard sounds outside the library window. She lifted the window and leaned out into the cold. There beneath the window, buried up to his waist in the deep snow, was her old friend Pudgey Bear.

Pudgey stood in the circle of light cast from the room behind Jeannie.

"Er-um, er-um, greetings, Miss Jeannie, and welcome to Crab Lake."

"Oh, Pudgey. How wonderful to see you—and all our friends." For she now saw back in the shadows behind Pudgey a large crowd of animal friends. Jeannie could make out the deer, pawing restlessly in the snow, the beavers, otters, woodchucks, and two polar bears.

Jeannie pointed. "Oh! There are Klondike and Snow!" The two polar bear cubs had found their way to Crab Lake from a plane crash near Manitowish Waters a few years back. "And look! There's the entire O'Possum family from Lynx Bay and the squirrels and moles and the owls. They are all here—all the friends!"

"Yes, we are all here," the animals shouted in unison.

"We are here," shouted Pudgey, "and we can talk now—so welcome and Merry Christmas!"

In the next two days, the animals were everywhere, shouting, squeaking, chattering, barking, hooting, and talking, helping Jeannie to hang decorations in places too hard to reach, stringing lights high in the trees, pulling tree branches through the snow down to the lake to prepare for Kaitlin's bonfire out on the ice. Log ends were placed by the deer and beavers in a circle in the deep snow to be used as seats beside a large campfire to be built outside the lower level between the new stone walls.

Inside the cabin, raccoons and moles, glasses carefully perched on their small noses, strung cranberries and popcorn on long pieces of string to decorate the tree. Jeannie marveled at how quickly their tiny black-and-pink fingers worked the string through the bright red berries and white popcorn. Under the tree, in the cup-shaped tree stand, the frogs stayed immersed in the water, which was their job to bring in from the snow outside without making a mess on the new floors. Higher up on the tree, the spiders did their part by weaving delicate, prismed webs as decorations in among the pine needles and the brightly colored baubles hung ever so dexterously by Hummer, the hummingbird.

The cabin was transformed by Jeannie's animal friends into a woodland extravaganza, never before seen at any Christmas. Mrs. Mole and all the little moles shuffled round the house serving birch-bark tea and pinecone pastries. Two fawns, still with their spots, spent most of their time curled up sleeping on the sofas, and the cardinals took turns posting themselves beautifully on the Christmas tree and among the pine boughs around the house to enhance the Christmas decorations.

"Wait till Kaitlin sees this," enthused Jeannie. "She won't believe it, and she'll talk and talk and talk with our friends until the owls tuck her into bed."

The day of the arrival of Jeannie's family was bright and sunny but bitterly cold. Snow lay deep around the cabin and deeper still out along South Crab Road.

Unfortunately, as Jeannie learned from the cardinals, the snow was so deep south of Manitowish Waters and Boulder Junction, especially around Trout Lake, that even the great snow ploughs of Villas County could not get through from Minocqua. Boulder Junction, added Klondike and Snow, who had been out exploring toward Fish Trap Lake, was literally buried up to the roofs of the houses.

"We couldn't even find Mad Dog Jake's to get some ice cream," they lamented. "And there weren't any snowmobiles out either—too deep," they shouted, jumping off the lakeside deck into snow over their heads.

"Oh dear," sighed Jeannie. "Something had to go wrong. It always does in winter up here. What to do? What to do?"

"To do? Who, who," chimed in Owlie and Owlette. "To do? Who, who, what to do, to do?"

Word of the impending Christmas disaster for Jeannie and her family quickly spread among the animals. Jeannie tried telephoning the airport, but the line was dead. She sat by the fire, wringing her hands.

Where was her family? Had their flights arrived at Wausau? Were they stuck in Chicago and Milwaukee? Was Christmas going to be ruined? Even Jason and Jodie seemed to be stuck in their house at Fish Trap, probably cut off by trees fallen over the road from the weight of the snow.

"Oh dear, what's to be done?" she cried. "We'd be marooned if we ventured out, lost and frozen in the deep drifts if it starts to snow again."

"Turn on the radio," suggested David. "There's sure to be weather advisories."

Jeannie rushed to the radio and, in a few minutes, discovered the worst. Northern Wisconsin had had the biggest snowstorm in its history. North of Merrill, the land was buried in drifts higher than the ploughs. Businesses and even the famous beer bars of Wisconsin were closed. There were no public services, electricity, or telephones in most northern counties. Wausau airport was open, but only for flights to and from the south.

Jeannie stepped outside in the dark, fighting back the tears. All the effort, the planning, the finishing and furnishing of the cabin, the carrying of boxes from London, the finding and delivering of special Christmas ornaments, the food, and the wonderful effort of her animal friends was for naught. Kaitlin wouldn't get to see the winter wonderland, and it wouldn't be a family Christmas at Molly Point after all.

Jeannie hadn't realized it, but she'd been thinking out loud. Suddenly, she saw that a number of her animal friends had gathered around her. Pudgey Bear stood with a worried look on his black, furry face. The smaller animals were circled around Jeannie's feet. The deer stood respectfully a little way back, their breath making small clouds of steam in the bitter cold. Above on the front lanterns perched Owlie and Owlette, and over on the old birch tree stood the eagle in perfect, imperial silence.

Jeannie heard a rustling sound from the hill running down to the back bay. Out of the darkness came old Belknap Beaver of Borden Lake, his large, fuzzy head bent forward in reflection. He stopped before her and leaned back on his thick black tail. All the fidgeting among the animals stopped.

"We face a serious situation." Belknap's deep voice resonated in the cold stillness of the evening. "Your family is all together at Wausau airport. They are safe and warm. But they can't move anywhere. I am advised by all my flying scouts and by the entire Wisconsin River beaver network that all roads are impassable."

Everyone listened, waiting for Belknap's next words. Jeannie could feel the disappointment rising in her breast.

"I have considered the matter from all angles, just as we beavers do before starting work on a new dam or before taking down a big tree."

"Yes," whispered Jeannie, "and what do you think?"

"I think we have one chance to bring your family to Molly Point before Christmas."

"How so?" Jeannie asked.

"By using the magic sleigh," intoned Belknap in his wise and balanced voice. "This will be difficult, however, because the sleigh has never traveled so far. We would need large numbers of deer posted at intervals along the way to relieve each group of deer as they pull the sleigh for miles and miles through the deep snow."

The crowd of animals gave a collective sigh. How could this be done?

"I am not sure that Mr. O'Possum of Lynx Bay, our esteemed friend and the driver of the sleigh, knows the way to Wausau. And there are many humans in Wausau who could interfere, especially if they discover that we animals can talk. We might all end up in zoos or circus sideshows."

These were serious matters, all the animals realized, and they looked questioningly at Jeannie for guidance.

"What to do, do, do—who, who, who," the owls hooted softly, repeating the refrain again and again.

A sense of gloom and discouragement settled over the small crowd. All of the animals were sad for Jeannie, who had now begun to cry.

"I can't possibly ask you to take the sleigh all the way to Wausau," Jeannie sighed. "It's too far, too dangerous. I can't bear to think of you being captured and taken to zoos and circuses. Oh dear, what a disaster that would be. We could never forgive ourselves. We shall

have to manage alone and hope the roads can be cleared in time for them to come after Christmas."

Silence. Disappointment. The animals realized that Jeannie was right. Wausau's world was too far from Crab Lake, a world that they knew from watching hunters in the autumn and speedboats in the summer was dangerous and destructive. They knew also, just as Jeannie had said, that all the animals belonged in the peaceful wilderness of Crab Lake in winter, happy and secure with their great and good friend Jeannie.

Gradually, all the animals but Pudgey Bear dispersed—some into the forest, some into the cabin to finish their various tasks. Jeannie remained on the large pine log, leaning against the towering snowdrift beside the front window. Light from the windows cast its soft glow on Pudgey. Neither could speak. There was nothing to say. Christmas Eve was only a day away, and now, Jeannie noticed through her tears, it was snowing again, tiny, sparkling flakes that drifted softly down.

Christmas Eve morning broke clear and cold. That morning in the bright sunshine, Jeannie made her way slowly through the waist-deep snow to the garage. The snow banks from repeated plowing on either side of the garage towered high over Jeannie's head. No animals were to be seen when she entered the garage, which would now no longer be needed.

When she came outside again, an enormous deer with massive antlers stood facing her. At first, she thought he was an elk because of his great size, and she was a little uneasy. Then she noticed Pudgey and Belknap standing to the side. Belknap stepped forward and said:

"This is Olympus, the master of all the deer herds in the Northwoods, and he has a secret message for you."

"Oh, what is it? And, er, delighted to meet you, sir," Jeannie stammered, realizing she had perhaps been too direct. Olympus stood tall and proud. He shook his antlers gently and cleared his throat with a great puff of frosty steam coming into the sunlight.

"I have some very important, some very unusual, some very special and quite surprisingly powerful friends to whom I have taken the liberty of speaking on your behalf about the sad Christmas plight of your family."

There was a long pause as Olympus let this information sink into Jeannie's consciousness. She said nothing. Pudgey and Belknap stood silent and wide-eyed.

"After consultations with them," he continued, "I am able to give you a simple message—on one condition."

"And what is that condition?" asked Jeannie, looking into the face of this great animal and noticing for the first time that, in addition to his antlers, he had a small and rather stylish beard.

"The condition is," Olympus revealed, "that you must ask no questions. Is that agreed?"

"Of course." Jeannie smiled. "I cannot think of what question I would have."

"In that case," intoned the great Olympus, "I have been asked to tell you to set your Christmas Eve dinner table for seventeen."

"What? What does this mean?" Jeannie turned to Pudgey and Belknap. As she did so, she heard a swooshing sound and felt a spray of snow across her face. When she turned back, Olympus had disappeared in a single leap over the high bank of snow, and no sign of him remained except his deep footprints in the snow before her.

Jeannie turned back to Pudgey and Belknap. "Do you know what this means?"

Belknap slowly shook his head and said, "I don't know. I don't know anything more than you do. Olympus just asked us to bring him here. That is all."

Christmas is a time of faith, a season of hope and renewal. Molly Point was no exception that day as sunset faded into dusk and dusk into the most beautifully clear twilight. The new moon was back again, lying on its side above the trees, so clear and bright that Jeannie was sure there was a man in the moon this night.

Keeping faith with Olympus, Jeannie had done exactly as he had instructed. She had set the table for seventeen with the help of Jodi, Jason, and David and had prepared dinner for the same number.

The candles were lit, the outside lights were all ablaze, Christmas music played softly, fires blazed, and a number of the smaller animals were milling about inside the cabin. Pudgey sat in the corner of the library, conversing with Badger and Mr. Woodchuck.

Dinner was ready; the clock struck ten. Jeannie sat patiently beside the window, looking up at Owlie and Owlette, perched high above her on the birch-bark canoe, their large, yellow eyes blinking slowly. They were listening. They were all listening. But not a sound.

Eleven o'clock. *Was dinner spoiled?* Jeannie worried. What does it all mean? Still the silence, and Jeannie began to feel sleepy.

Suddenly, the owls stirred. "Shhsst," they said and cocked their large, fuzzy heads. Jeannie knew owls could hear for miles, but what did they hear?

Next came a soft thump on the roof, just above the fireplace. Jeannie thought she heard bells, then a deep chuckle, almost a laugh. Snow slid off the roof past the window. Jeannie jumped up from her chair and raced to the door. *What is happening?* she wondered as she grasped the heavy latch and swung the big door open.

Now she heard a swoosh and the sound of bells. But then she heard the clear and unmistakable voice of Kaitlin.

"Hey, get us down from here. Oops, we're sliding. Whoa! Hang on to the chimney, everyone!"

Jeannie looked up, and to her astonishment she saw the family huddled in the snow around the chimney, hanging on for dear life.

"Here we are," shouted Kathleen.

"In time for Christmas dinner," called Jeannie. "Come on, just slide down. The snow's so deep you can't possibly get hurt. Except for you, Nana—hang on to the chimney while Jason gets the ladder."

Kaitlin was the first to come sliding down the roof. Yikes! Up to her neck in snow. Then Kathleen, Randee, Matt, Adam, John, Tom, and little Ben. Everyone landed in deep snow and climbed out laughing and brushing off.

"Oh, excuse me, Mrs. Mulford." It was Lambi. "I am here too. Delighted, I'm sure, but, speaking for myself, could you please pull me out?"

"How did you get here?" cried Jeannie. "How did it happen?"

Now Dorothy was down—shivering, but safely down and heading inside for the fire.

"Our luggage is at the Wausau airport," Randee explained, "but here we are."

"We got a ride," shouted Kaitlin, "in a beautiful sleigh with eight great reindeer."

"No," exclaimed Jeannie.

"Yes," cried Kathleen, Kaitlin, and Randee all together.

"We flew over the trees," shouted Kaitlin, "and above the lakes. And it wasn't cold. We saw all the stars and the moon. And you know who drove the sleigh?"

"I think I can guess," said Jeannie, and she looked up at the sky just in time to see a sleigh, eight reindeer, and a small plump figure cross in front of the moon.

"Yes, I'm sure I know who brought you to Crab Lake for Christmas."

About the Author

$\mathcal{F}$or David Mulford and his wife, Jeannie, the winter holidays would not be complete without their visits to the beautiful Wisconsin waters of Crab Lake. These magical journeys provide the inspiration for David's whimsical tales. For the last twenty-eight years, David's Christmas gift to Jeannie, no matter where they've been in the world, has been a story of Christmas at Crab Lake. For another such tale, read the first book in the series, *Jeannie's Crab Lake Christmas*.

In addition to writing, David has a PhD from Oxford University, serves as a Distinguished Visiting Fellow at the Hoover Institute at Stanford University, and has enjoyed a long and notable career in international finance and diplomacy, serving as undersecretary for international affairs in the US Treasury, as well as the United States ambassador to India from 2004 to 2009. When not traveling, David and Jeannie reside in Paradise Valley, Arizona.

About the Illustrator

$\mathcal{C}$hristine Cathers Donohue resides in New Jersey with her husband and two children. She has a BFA from the University of the Arts as well as a wealth of experience illustrating greeting cards and producing award-winning fine art paintings. Christine dedicates this book to her parents, Frank and Ethel, for supporting a dreamer.